I'm
(aLMosT)
ALWAYS KIND

Designed by Nicola Butler
Cover design by Lucy Wain

Usborne Publishing, Usborne House, 83-85 Saffron Hill, London EC1N 8RT, England

I'm (aLMosT) ALWAYS KiND

Anna Milbourne

Illustrated by Åsa Gilland

My mommy told me that being KIND is the most important thing in all the world.

"More important than being the fastest runner?" I asked. "Or than knowing all the answers?"

"Even more important than those," she said.

"Then it is very lucky," I said quickly, "that I am ALWAYS kind."

...sharing
my candy...

Being KIND means...

...helping my little sister
reach things from
a high shelf...

...putting away
the breakfast
things...

...trying to cheer
people up when
they feel sad.

But sometimes when I am kind,
it doesn't work out the way I want it to...

"Hey, New Kid, I like your crazy hair!"

Why did she look so sad when I gave her a nice compliment?

Why was Mr. Williams so mad about me being kind to snails?

"Here you go, little snails: a nice dinner for you. Eat up all the flowers!"

"Hey! Stop that!"

And when I invent a great game for me and my sister to play...

"Let's be GIANTS jumping on castles!"

...she screams,
"WAAAAAAAH!
YOU'RE SO MEAN!!!"

And I feel mad
and bad and sad.

I ONLY
meant to
be KIND.

I helped fix my sister's sandcastles. And afterwards,
I told Mommy that I hadn't meant to be mean.

Mommy understood. "But what YOU think is nice isn't
always the same as what someone else thinks is nice.
Sometimes, to be kind to someone, you have
to walk around in their shoes first."

So I tried it...

"YOU RUINED MOMMY'S SHOES!
She's going to be so mad!"

It didn't work.
Now I didn't feel like being
kind to ANYONE.

Mommy wasn't mad. She smiled instead. "I didn't mean REAL shoes," she said. "I meant trying to put yourself in someone else's place. If you imagine how they might feel, you might see what could make them happy."
"I'm sorry about your shoes," I told her.

She gave me a hug, and it unrumpled my feelings and made ME feel happy...

Mommy is KIND.

"This is what it feels like when someone is kind to you," I thought. So I decided to try again.

Before I put snails on Mr. Williams' garden the next day,
I tried to imagine how he feels about his garden.

He LOVES those flowers.

So I thought it might be kinder to look after them.

"Off you go,
little snails.
You can eat the weeds."

"Thank you!"

When I thought of a fun game to play with my sister, I tried imagining how she might see it first.

What would she think of a great, big water fight...?

If I was in her place, I guess I wouldn't want all my paintings to get soaking wet...

sploosh!

So instead I said,
"Can I play too?" (Even though
I could think of games
I'd rather play.)

But after I painted pictures with my sister,
she played lots of my favorite games with me.

"Being kind is GREAT," I thought.

But some people are hard to be kind to...
At school, I found the new kid sitting on her own. She looked really grumpy. Everyone else was playing and having fun, so I sat down by her and asked, "Do you want to play tag?"
"No," she said.
"Skipping?" I asked.
"NO," she said.

In the end I said, "I want to be kind to you,
but I don't know how... What will make you happy?"
She looked at me. "I like soccer?" she said.

HOP

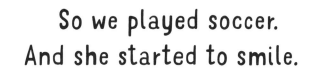

So we played soccer.
And she started to smile.

So did I.

Then I realized something.
Being kind doesn't just make OTHER people happy...

It makes
YOU happy too!

Kindness makes you feel warm and sunshiny.
And when you feel that way, you feel like
being kind to someone else.

"Oh no, are you ok?
Want me to help you up?"

"Thanks!"

"You dropped these!
Here you go..."

So the kindness
gets
passed
on...

Being kind is sometimes easy and sometimes hard. But it's really important to try.

And because it's the imPORTant-est thing in the world,

I am (almost) always KIND.